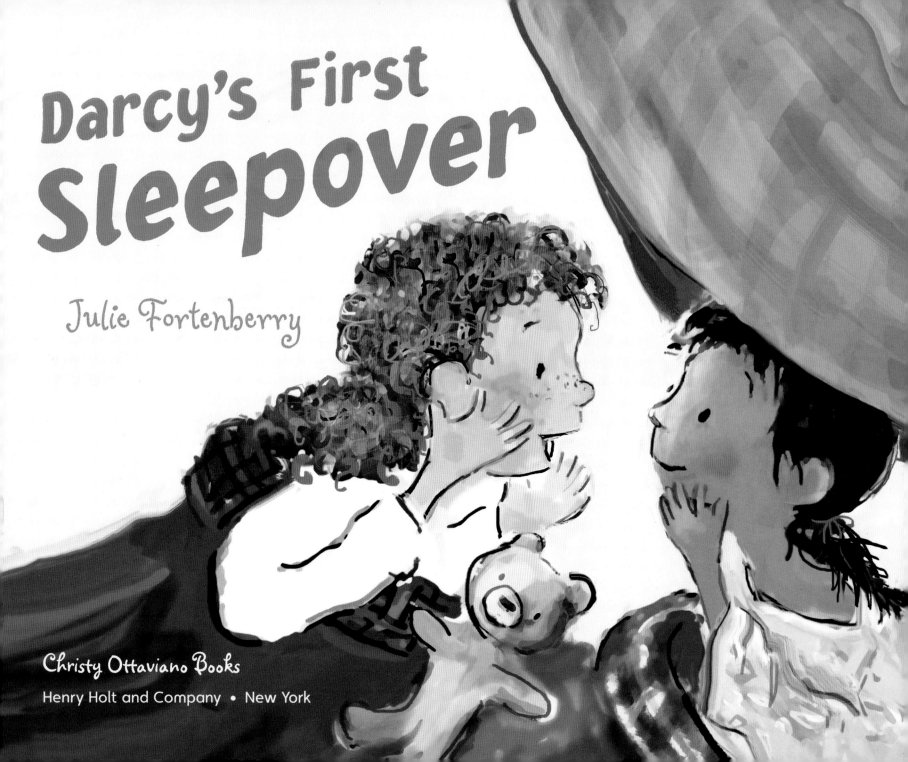

Darcy's First Sleepover

Julie Fortenberry

Christy Ottaviano Books

Henry Holt and Company • New York

Henry Holt and Company, *Publishers since 1866*
Henry Holt® is a registered trademark of Macmillan Publishing Group, LLC.
120 Broadway, New York, NY 10271
mackids.com

Library of Congress Cataloging-in-Publication Data
Names: Fortenberry, Julie, 1956- author, illustrator.
Title: Darcy's first sleepover / Julie Fortenberry.
Description: First edition. | New York : Henry Holt and Company, 2021. |
Audience: Ages 3-7. | Audience: Grades K-1. | Summary: When Darcy spends her first
night away from home she is a little apprehensive, but when the sun comes up
and breakfast is on the table she realizes sleepovers can be a lot of fun.
Identifiers: LCCN 2020038060 | ISBN 9781250755902 (hardcover)
Subjects: CYAC: Sleepovers—Fiction.
Classification: LCC PZ7.1.F664 Dar 2021 | DDC [E]—dc23
LC record available at https://lccn.loc.gov/2020038060

Our books may be purchased in bulk for promotional, educational, or business use.
Please contact your local bookseller or the Macmillan Corporate and Premium Sales Department
at (800) 221-7945 ext. 5442 or by email at MacmillanSpecialMarkets@macmillan.com.

First Edition, 2021 / Design by Liz Dresner
The illustrations were painted digitally.
Printed in China by Hung Hing Off-set Printing Co. Ltd.,
Heshan City, Guangdong Province

1 3 5 7 9 10 8 6 4 2

For Don, who's always there for

Annie, John, and me

Dressed in her comfy polka-dot pajamas, Darcy was almost ready for bed. She brushed her teeth with her strawberry toothpaste.

Then, snug in her bed with Little Cat, her favorite stuffed animal, she was all set for a bedtime story.

She knew the story had a happy ending. But she always got nervous when the waves almost knocked Little Cat right out of her boat.

When the storm clouds drifted away and Little Cat was safe, Darcy could relax.

Tonight, like every night, she switched off her lamp as her dad turned on the kitchen light. And she dozed off listening to her dad wash the dishes.

The next night she went to visit her cousin, Kayla. She'd never been to Kayla's house before, and it smelled kind of spicy, like pizza.

They ate outside and had
celery with peanut butter on it.

And they had cookies in Kayla's room.

"I'm not allowed to eat cookies in my room," said Darcy.

"Time to go," called Darcy's dad a little later.

"Can Darcy spend the night?" asked Kayla. "She can wear one of my nightgowns!"

"You and Kayla can have a sleepover, and I'll be back in the morning. Does that sound like fun?" Dad whispered. Darcy nodded yes.

Kayla gave Darcy a nightgown to wear. It was a little too big. And kind of scratchy.

She gave her a new toothbrush and peppermint toothpaste. Darcy wasn't sure that she liked peppermint toothpaste.

"I have strawberry toothpaste at my house," she said.

They got to stay up late and make a tent in the living room. They lined up all of Kayla's stuffed animals. A baby bear named Charlotte was Kayla's favorite.

It was fun, but it made Darcy miss Little Cat.

Could she go to sleep without her?

"Can I call my dad?" asked Darcy.

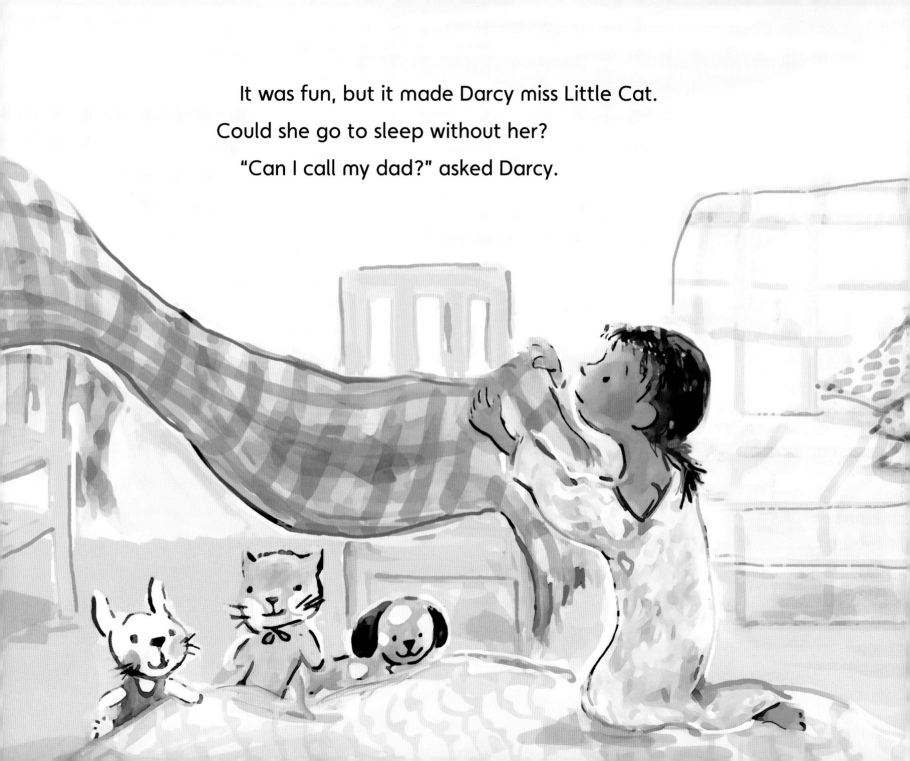

"Hello, Daddy. How is Little Cat?"

"She's purring just like the rhyme in the story. How does that go again?" he asked.

Darcy sang: "Cat begins to purr when the storm clouds drift away. The moon shines down on her, till the dawn begins the day."

"Little Cat will be just fine," said her dad.

"I know," said Darcy, and they both wished the other good night.

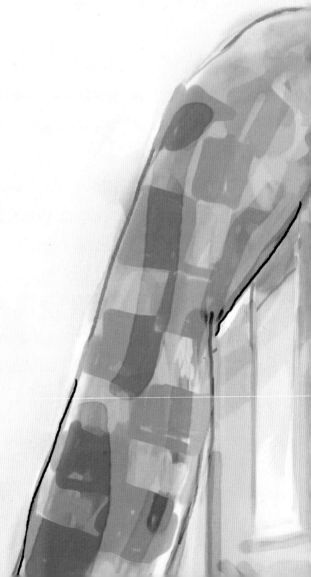

At bedtime, Kayla and Darcy got into sleeping bags in the tent. Kayla sang silly songs and told stories about Charlotte.

But after a while, Kayla yawned and turned over, and Darcy's aunt turned off the lights.

"Kayla?" whispered Darcy.
But Kayla didn't answer.

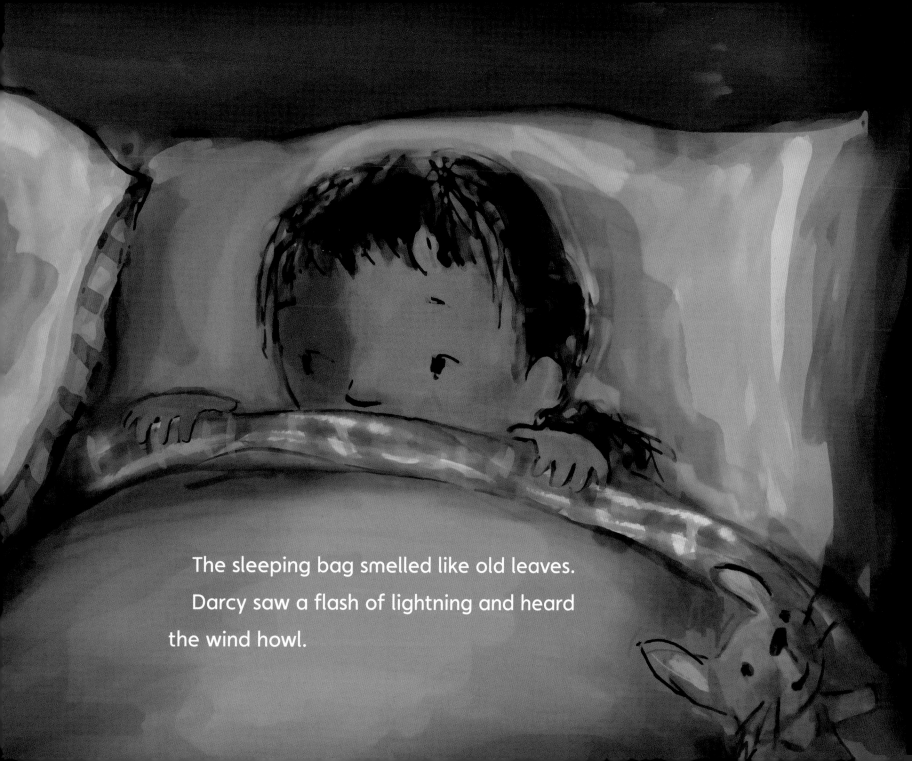

The sleeping bag smelled like old leaves.
Darcy saw a flash of lightning and heard
the wind howl.

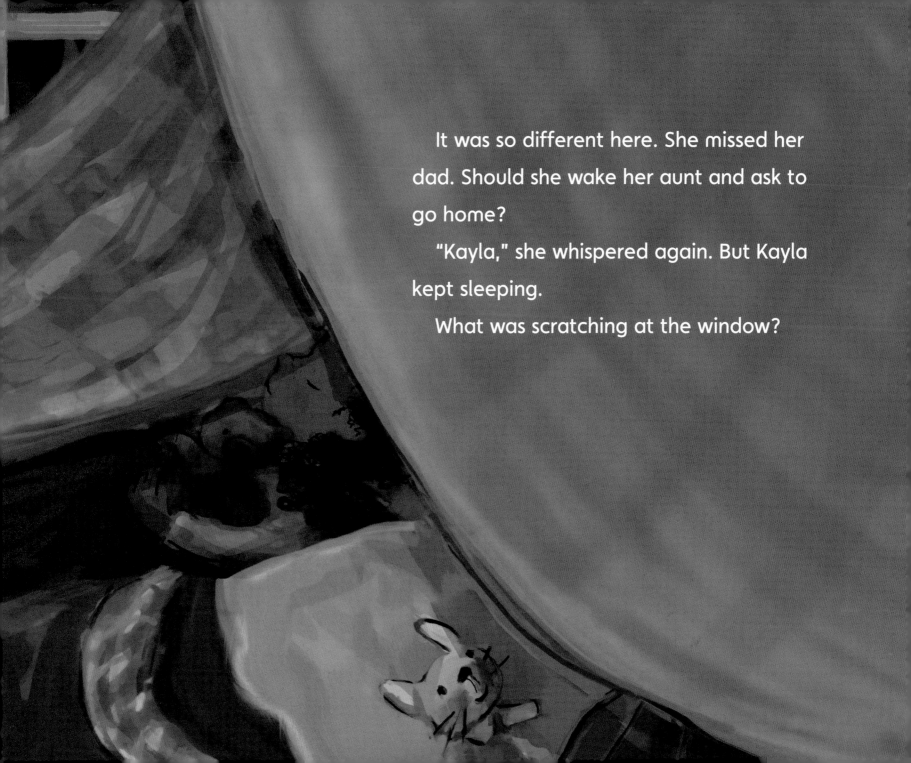

It was so different here. She missed her dad. Should she wake her aunt and ask to go home?

"Kayla," she whispered again. But Kayla kept sleeping.

What was scratching at the window?

It was just the branches and the wind.
Darcy watched the storm clouds drift away,
and the moon shone down on her just like
it did on Little Cat.

She crawled back into the sleeping bag and put her head down on her pillow. Darcy felt like she was floating, and she couldn't keep her eyes open any longer.

When Darcy opened her eyes, the sun
was up! She'd made it through the night,
and the morning smelled like pancakes!
"Hi, Sleepyhead!" said Kayla.

They ate breakfast and planned another sleepover.

"This time, at my house," said Darcy.

"But I've never slept at anyone else's house before," said Kayla.

"Don't worry," said Darcy.

"It might be a little scary at first.

But it's really fun."

Author's Note

When my daughter, Annie, was young, she tried sleepovers a few times before making it through the night. On her first attempt, my husband picked her up before dawn and she said, "I just don't know how people do it!"

Peer pressure was a big motivator, so very little nudging was needed for her to keep trying. She didn't have a cousin and aunt nearby. But like Darcy, her first sleepover attempt was in the home of a good friend and a familiar adult.

We let her know that we were just a phone call away, even if just to say good night. And since she missed her bedtime ritual—arranging stuffed animals around her pillow—her pillow and stuffed animal Minni were sleepaway necessities.

As Annie got older, Minni stayed in her backpack (it was comforting just to know she was close by). We hosted sleepovers where bedtime routines were forgotten. But the most important thing that my husband and I did was simply wait.

When Annie finally spent an entire night away from home, she did it on her own schedule. On the car ride home, I could tell that she was proud. And like Darcy, she was planning the next sleepover.

Minni